Uphoff 2001

S0-DJZ-408

The Secret Of Dinosaur Bog

More Monsterish Fun with C.D. Bitesky, Howie Wolfner, Elisa and Frankie Stein, and Danny Keegan
From Avon Camelot

THE FIFTH GRADE MONSTERS SERIES

M IS FOR MONSTER
BORN TO HOWL
THE PET OF FRANKENSTEIN
THERE'S A BATWING IN MY LUNCHBOX
Z IS FOR ZOMBIE
MONSTER MASHERS
THINGS THAT GO BARK IN THE PARK
YUCKERS!
THE MONSTER IN CREEPS HEAD BAY
HOW TO BE A VAMPIRE IN ONE EASY LESSON
ISLAND OF THE WEIRD
WEREWOLF, COME HOME
MONSTER BOY
TROLL PATROL

Avon Books are available at special quantity discounts for bulk purchases for sales promotions, premiums, fund raising or educational use. Special books, or book excerpts, can also be created to fit specific needs.

For details write or telephone the office of the Director of Special Markets, Avon Books, Dept. FP, 1350 Avenue of the Americas, New York, New York 10019, 1-800-238-0658.

The Secret Of Dinosaur Bog

Mel Gilden

Illustrated by John Pierard

A GLC BOOK

AN AVON CAMELOT BOOK

If you purchased this book without a cover, you should be aware that this book is stolen property. It was reported as "unsold and destroyed" to the publisher, and neither the author nor the publisher has received any payment for this "stripped book."

THE SECRET OF DINOSAUR BOG is an original publication of Avon Books. This work has never before appeared in book form.

AVON BOOKS
A division of
The Hearst Corporation
1350 Avenue of the Americas
New York, New York 10019

Text and illustrations copyright © 1991 by General Licensing Company, Inc.
Published by arrangement with General Licensing Company, Inc.
Developed by Byron Preiss and Dan Weiss
Library of Congress Catalog Card Number: 91-92047
ISBN: 0-380-76308-7
RL: 4.4

All rights reserved, which includes the right to reproduce this book or portions thereof in any form whatsoever except as provided by the U.S. Copyright Law. For information address General Licensing Company, Inc., 24 West 25th Street, New York, New York 10010.

First Avon Camelot Printing: October 1991

CAMELOT TRADEMARK REG. U.S. PAT. OFF. AND IN OTHER COUNTRIES, MARCA REGISTRADA, HECHO EN U.S.A.

Printed in the U.S.A.

OPM   10 9 8 7 6 5 4 3 2 1

Chapter One

The Things You Find in an Attic

Breathing hard, Danny Keegan ran up the front steps of his house and turned to see how far ahead he was of his sister, Barbara, and their neighbor, Ryan Webler. They had raced the last block home from school and Danny could see that the other two were a good quarter block behind him.

Ryan was a pretty fast runner, so the only explanation for his staying with Barbara was that he didn't want her to feel bad when she lost. Danny would have stayed with her himself if Barbara hadn't been his sister.

Parked in front of the Keegan house was the white Oldsmobile that belonged to Danny's grampa Keegan. It was an enormous car made from vast acres of gently curved sheet metal. It looked as if it had been inflated, like a balloon. But Danny knew from having ridden in it that the car was as strong as a tank. Gramps had been driving it for as long as Danny could remember.

The presence of the car meant that Gramps had

1

already arrived. Danny and Barbara had suspected he would have, which was why they had started to run in the first place. Danny had an urge to go inside, but he and Barbara had made a solemn pact that whoever arrived home first would wait for the other.

As Ryan and Barbara dashed up the walk, Danny cried, "I win."

"No fair," Barbara grumbled. "You run too fast."

Barbara's remarks often puzzled Danny, but this one was exceptional. Ryan said, "*You* ran as fast as you could."

"Not as fast as him," Barbara said accusingly.

"Gramps is here," Danny said, hoping to change the subject to one he understood.

Barbara grinned and pushed past him into the house, leaving him alone with Ryan. Danny was eager to enter too, but he said to Ryan, "So, what are you going to do on vacation?"

"It's only three days. Just enough time to get my clip file in order."

Ryan wanted to be a writer when he grew up. He'd been clipping stories out of newspapers ever since his mom would let him hold a scissors, and he kept them in shoe boxes organized by subject.

"Have fun," said Danny as he glanced over his shoulder. Laughter came from inside the house.

"You too. But I guess you will. You've been talking about your grandfather for weeks."

"He's a great guy."

"I'll expect a full report," Ryan said and went away.

When Danny entered the house, everyone was standing around the living room admiring Barbara, who was talking about her ballet lessons and attempting to twist her feet into the correct positions. She actually had had only one lesson so far, but she had learned all the French words for the way you placed your feet and for the different parts of the weird outfit she wore. Danny thought it was all pretty sappy, but when he'd told Gilly Finn about it, she'd gotten dreamy eyed.

Gilly was one of Danny's monster friends. She had long blond hair held back by combs in the shape of seashells, and in the right light, you could almost see her delicate scales and the wispy fins at her wrists and ankles. She was the daughter of one of the Fabulous Finn Sisters. Show business was her life. Even ballet, evidently.

At the moment, Gramps was holding Barbara's hand while she tried to stand on the toes of one foot. Gramps was a little shorter and rounder than his son, Danny's father. He wore a short-sleeved cotton shirt of simple pattern and wide dark blue pants. The little hair he had left was white and wound in tiny curls over his ears and around the back of his head. He never quite stood up straight.

"Danny," Gramps shouted when he saw Danny, and they hugged. Gramps smelled like some kind of after-shave that had to be as old as he was. The odor was heavy, warm, and sweet, and it reminded Danny of comfortable old-fashioned barbershops.

"I've really been looking forward to this," Gramps said to Danny and Barbara as he rubbed his hands together. "What'll it be first? The ice cream store? The movie house? The wax museum? Cheapo City?" He winked.

"Gramps," Mrs. Keegan said in warning. But she was smiling too.

To Danny and Barbara, Gramps said, "Pay no attention to her. She's just an old stick-in-the-mud."

"You'll spoil them rotten," Mr. Keegan said.

"So what? I spoiled *you* rotten and *you* turned out all right." He cocked an eye at Mr. Keegan and finished, "More or less."

Everybody laughed and Mr. Keegan looked embarrassed.

"Besides," Gramps said, "what's the good of being rich if you can't spend the money on people you like?" He shook a finger in Danny's face and said, "Save your money, boy. And invest wisely, and someday *you'll* be able to spend money on *your* grandchildren."

Danny could barely imagine being in high school, let alone having grandchildren.

Gramps looked off into the distance and said, "Did I ever tell you how I almost lost everything during the Great Depression?"

"Often," Mr. Keegan said.

They all laughed again, and when they were finished, Mrs. Keegan said, "I have an idea. Maybe Gramps can identify some of that old stuff in the attic."

"Old stuff?" asked Gramps. "Attic?" He crinkled up his eyes as if he were thinking hard.

"Trunks of it," Mrs. Keegan said.

"What a wonderful idea," Gramps said and quickly organized Danny and Barbara into a military column. "Onward, troops," called Gramps as he marched them toward the stairway.

Feeling a little foolish, Danny grinned and did his

part. But he wondered what the big draw of the attic was. He'd much rather have gone to a movie, or even for a walk around the park. Just strolling with Gramps was an adventure. He always noticed stuff that other people missed and he had strange ideas about it. Danny remembered one time on vacation in Los Angeles when Gramps explained about the little man in the Walk–Don't Walk sign.

Gramps had said, "First we see his whole body as he takes a step. Then we see just his hand. How do you think he moved from one position to the other so fast?"

"Maybe there are two guys," Danny said, "one with a hand and the other with a body."

Gramps thought over the theory and agreed that Danny might be right. Danny decided being right about this was unlikely but it didn't matter. Being silly with Gramps was fun.

Before they'd gotten halfway up the stairs, the front doorbell rang and Barbara ran down to get it. Gilly Finn came in with Frankie and Elisa Stein.

Frankie and Elisa were the two biggest kids in the fifth grade, and Frankie was probably the smartest. The Steins had bolts in their necks, and with his own eyes, Danny had seen them shoot big sparks from their fingers. Like Gilly, they were monsters, but of a different kind.

Danny was not very good at making introductions, but he managed to tell Gramps everybody's name, and Gramps shook hands all around. "Always delighted to meet the friends of my grandchildren."

"We are also delighted," Elisa said in her German

accent. Except when a scientific subject came up, Elisa did most of the talking for herself and for Frankie.

While Barbara dragged her up the stairs to show off her ballet stuff, Elisa said, "You are so lucky you can dance. I am—in the Old Country we say *klutz*."

"Same word here," Gilly said.

"Well, it looks as if we lost Barbara," Gramps said. "Are we about to lose Danny?"

Danny looked at Frankie and Gilly and said, "We were just going upstairs to clean the attic."

"Ah," said Frankie and nodded.

"Hey, radical," Gilly cried. "I love attics."

"You do?" said Danny.

"Sure. Never know what you'll find in an attic."

"Very well, then," said Gramps. "Onward!"

They all tromped up the stairs with Mr. and Mrs. Keegan coming last. Gramps stopped in front of a door in the upstairs hallway that they almost never used, and opened it. He switched on a light and beyond the door Danny saw a steep wooden staircase with another door at the top. The paint on the top door was spotted and faded and cracked, as if it had been applied about the time Gramps was a kid.

Footsteps sounded loud and hollow in the narrow stairwell. When he reached the top, Gramps turned back and chuckled at the kids evilly. "You never know what you'll find in an attic," he said in a voice straight out of an old horror movie.

Danny hoped that Frankie and Gilly wouldn't be offended. They hated old horror movies because they gave monsters such a bad name. But neither Frankie nor Gilly seemed to have noticed.

Gramps turned the door handle and slowly pushed open the door. It squeaked badly. Beyond the door was a black, door-shaped hole. The attic seemed to swallow light. Gramps felt around for a light switch and flicked it on.

Looking into the attic was like looking through the side of a swimming pool filled with pale yellow water. Ominous shapes stood in the corners with stacks of magazines at their feet. Broken tennis rackets and an unstrung guitar hung from the rafters. A rack of ancient coats stuck into the center of the room as if it had been caught trying to escape. Everything was covered with a fine layer of dust. A dust bunny rolled across the floor in the faint breeze that blew in through the open door.

"Hm," Gramps said like a dentist investigating a mouth.

Mr. and Mrs. Keegan started in a corner, sorting magazines. From the conversation, Danny could tell that each of his parents had a different approach to cleaning out an attic.

"Look at these old magazines," Mr. Keegan said. "*Collier's, Liberty.* They don't write stories like this anymore." He flipped through a copy of *Collier's* and began to sneeze from all the dust that exploded from it.

"Absolute junk," Mrs. Keegan said. "We'll be lucky to get ten cents a pound for it."

Meanwhile, Danny, Frankie, and Gilly followed Gramps as he wandered around the attic touching this and that. "Here's a Moxie bottle," He held up a yellow soft drink bottle with a dead cockroach inside. "Very popular stuff. Refreshing too, if you develop a taste for it."

7

"Do they still make it?" Gilly asked.

"So I hear. It's hard to find, that's for sure. Mostly, it's gone the way of the dodo, radio drama, and the slide rule."

"I have a slide rule," Frankie said.

"Do you ever use it?" Gramps asked.

"Not very often," Frankie said and looked embarrassed. "I would not keep it at all except that it was given to me by my father. I use a pocket calculator."

"Moxie is the slide rule of soft drinks," Gramps said and put down the bottle.

"Are you looking for something in particular, Gramps?" Danny said.

"Not exactly. Not as such." He turned his head as if he'd heard a noise and marched over to something covered by an old blanket. He looked down at the blanket for a long time before he started to gently pull it off.

"It is a trunk," Frankie said.

"Very good," Gramps said. "See if you can open it."

Frankie got down on his knees and studied the front. "It is not locked," he said, and lifted the lid with both hands.

Inside the trunk was some sheet music. Old stuff like "The Sidewalks of New York," "Fascinating Rhythm," "By the Light of the Silvery Moon," and something called "Lida Rose." The sheets were tattered like old flags and they had been fixed again and again with cellophane tape. But the tape had long since fallen away, leaving behind yellow stripes. Gilly picked up "Alexander's Ragtime Band," and began to sing. Her voice filled the room, and when she was done, everybody applauded.

"Very nice," Elisa said.

"Radical," Barbara said.

The two girls stood in the doorway looking in with big eyes. "What else did you find?" Barbara said.

"A trunk," Frankie said.

"Indeed," said Gramps, and huffing and hurrumphing, got down on his knees next to Frankie. Everybody gathered around as he pulled out a burlap bag the size of a table lamp. Gramps handled the heavy package as if he knew what was inside and that it was made of glass.

"What is it, Dad?" Mr. Keegan said.

"How would I know?" Gramps said.

"How, indeed?" Mr. Keegan said.

Gramps hurrumphed again and began to unwrap the burlap. A moment later he set a very strange object on the floor.

"It looks like a dinosaur," Barbara said.

"Sort of," Gilly said.

They were both right. It looked like a one-eyed dinosaur that had been carved out of rock either in a great hurry or by somebody who didn't have much experience. It was rough and crude, and the single eye looked like a big clear marble.

"The Eye of Brooklyn," Gramps said as if talking in church.

"Did you put it there?" Mr. Keegan said.

"If I did, it was a long time ago." He turned the statue around in his hands, feeling it all over.

9

"May I?" said Frankie.

Gramps handed the statue to him and he looked hard at the Eye. Frankie said, "I believe this eye is made from meteoric quartz."

"Meteoric?" Gilly said.

"It is made from a meteor."

"Wow," said Danny. "A rock from space."

Frankie handed the statue back to Gramps, who set it on the floor with a thump. When he did, the Eye fell out of the dinosaur's socket, rolled a short way across the warped floor, and came to a stop. A second later, the front doorbell rang.

"I'll get it," Mrs. Keegan said, and ran out of the attic.

Frankie picked up the Eye and tried to reinsert it in the socket, but it wouldn't stay. "Is there some trick?" he asked.

"Maybe," Gramps said. "I don't remember."

Mrs. Keegan's voice came up the stairs. "Danny, I want to see you down here right now." She did not sound happy.

"Danny's in trouble," Barbara said confidentially and with a certain delight.

Danny agreed with her, though he had no idea what terrible thing he might have done. He went down from the attic and then downstairs to the foyer.

Standing before the front door with Mrs. Keegan and a couple of battered suitcases was Stevie Brickwald. Stevie was wearing his innocent look, which meant that something was definitely up.

Mrs. Keegan said, "Stevie says he's come to stay

10

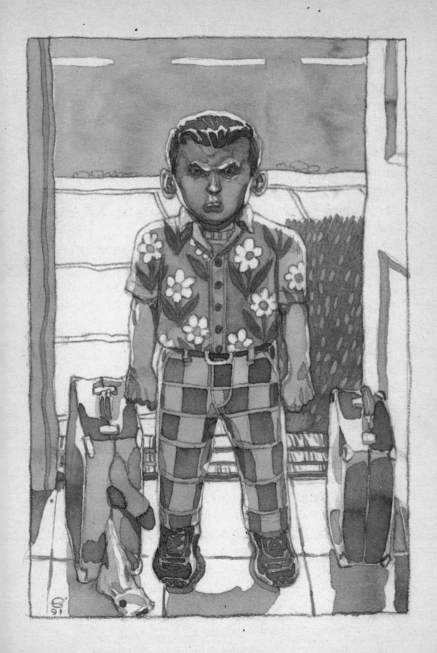

with us while his parents are out of town. And he says that you told him it would be OK.''

"Huh?'' was all Danny could think of to say. Stevie Brickwald was the fifth grade bully and the last person in the universe he'd invite to sleep over.

Chapter Two

Not Just Another Marble

Stevie said, "That's what you said, Danny."

"I never did."

Stevie started to sniffle. He said, "My parents are out of town and you won't let me stay here and I'll have to lie in a cardboard box in an empty lot with all the poor homeless people."

"Take it easy, Stevie," Mrs. Keegan said. "Wait right here."

While Stevie continued to sniffle, Mrs. Keegan took Danny by the arm and led him into the kitchen. "OK, Danny," she said. "What is this all about?"

"I really don't know, Mom. Really. If I was going to ask somebody to stay over, would it be Stevie Brickwald?"

His mom bit her lip and frowned. Danny had told his parents about Stevie. Mrs. Keegan could not possibly believe that Danny would associate with him voluntarily. She saw how shocked and horrified Danny was by Stevie's appearance at their door. Stevie's main form of recreation was making threats that he carried out just often enough to make them worth taking seriously.

"If you didn't invite him, what's he doing here?"

"Haven't a clue, Mom."

She pushed open the door a crack and looked out. A moment later she let the door swing closed and said, "He's just standing there."

Danny said nothing. There was nothing to say. He wasn't in the habit of pounding information out of people, but Stevie had definitely crossed the line and Danny would do what he had to to find out what Stevie had in mind.

"Gramps is staying in the guest room," Mrs. Keegan said.

Not even Stevie Brickwald should have to stay anywhere all by himself, whether it was in a cardboard box or in his own house. Unhappily, Danny said, "I guess he could stay in my room with me."

"That seems appropriate," Mrs. Keegan said.

That settled the matter, though not to the satisfaction of either of them. When they went back into the foyer, Mrs. Keegan said, "Where did your parents go, Stevie? How long will they be gone?"

Stevie looked sincerely confused. He said, "I don't know. It all happened pretty fast. The truth is, I don't even remember how I got here."

"Are you all right?" Mrs. Keegan said and rested her hand on Stevie's forehead.

"Hey," said Stevie, suddenly his own combative self again. "You don't have to worry about me."

Danny thought it unwise to point out that only

moments before Stevie had been sniveling about being left alone. The two of them went upstairs. Danny got down his sleeping bag and helped Stevie spread it on the bedroom floor. "It's an OK room, Keegan," Stevie said as he looked around.

Danny ignored the comment. He sat down on the bed and said, "So, what's the real story, Stevie?"

"Real story?"

"Yeah. Not even you just show up on somebody's doorstep with some vague excuse."

Stevie said angrily, "None of your beeswax."

Danny stood up. "You're staying in my room. My parents are going to feed you. I guess that makes it my beeswax." His heart was pounding and he felt his blood rushing. He didn't often have the nerve to speak to Stevie this way.

Stevie held up his fist but Danny didn't move. Stevie lowered his fist and the rest of him sagged. He said, "Keegan, I really don't know."

Gramps came into the room followed by Frankie, who carried the dinosaur statue. Behind them were Elisa, Barbara, and Gilly.

"I hear we have another guest in the house," Gramps said. He and Stevie introduced themselves and even shook hands, though Stevie looked uncomfortable doing it.

"We brought you the dinosaur statue," Gramps said. Frankie put it on the floor in a corner and handed the Eye to Danny.

"Thanks," said Danny. "But why?"

"For safekeeping," Barbara said. "I told him it would be just as safe in *my* room."

Gramps said, "I just thought a stone dinosaur would clash with all your pretty ballet equipment."

Barbara thought that over, and before she could give him an argument, Gramps distracted her by offering to take everybody, including Stevie, for ice cream.

When the cheering stopped, Danny said, "We'll be down in a minute." Everybody left, and he set the Eye on the floor next to the dinosaur statue. He said to Stevie, "You really don't know what you're doing here?"

"That's what I said, isn't it?"

"OK," Danny said. "Just don't forget whose room this is."

"Yeah," said Stevie. "And don't *you* forget who's the guest."

Gramps's presence seemed to make everything run smoothly. Everybody was on best behavior, and even Stevie didn't give him much trouble. At dinner that evening Stevie made a fuss about eating his green beans, and Mrs. Keegan made it clear that anybody who lived in her house was required to eat green beans whenever they were served.

"Looks like we're stuck," Gramps said and took a big mouthful of them.

At bedtime, Danny picked up the Eye of Brooklyn while Stevie put on his pajamas. "It's just a big dumb marble," Stevie said.

Danny had to admit that Stevie was probably right. He tried to put the Eye back into the socket, but it kept slipping out. "Must be some kind of trick," Danny said.

"Let me try," Stevie said.

Reluctantly, Danny handed over the Eye, and Stevie attempted to force it into the socket of the dinosaur statue.

"Don't break it," Danny said.

"Stupid statue," Stevie said. "I had a model kit like it once. Nothing would fit."

"What did you do?"

"I hammered it to bits."

"That taught it a lesson, I guess," Danny said. "Don't hammer the Eye."

"I ain't no barbarian, Keegan." He lobbed the Eye back.

They heard a sound and they both looked around.

"What was that?" Stevie said.

"Sounds like thunder."

The sound continued. As it got louder the thunder broke into separate beats, as if a herd of big animals were running toward them from the horizon.

"Strange neighborhood you got here, Keegan."

Danny would have run downstairs to where Gramps and his parents were watching TV, but he didn't have time. He and Stevie yelled, "Yikes!" as a ghostly pink dinosaur galloped in through the wall at one end of Danny's room. It was followed by a blue dinosaur, and then a green one. An entire herd came after that in a confusion of birthday cake colors. Each dinosaur was transparent, and they ran on a level three feet above the floor.

"Mom! Dad! Gramps!" Danny cried as he and Stevie looked on wild-eyed and tried to stay out of the way. The dinosaurs ran in through one wall, across the room,

and out the wall opposite. It looked as if they were coming from the bathroom and going into Barbara's room.

Wherever they were going, they were in a big hurry. They raised no dust and disturbed nothing. As far as Danny could tell, the dinosaurs thought they were running across some empty prehistoric plain.

The hall door opened just as the last of the ghost dinosaurs went through the wall. Mrs. Keegan was about to say something when Danny cried, "Listen."

As they all listened to the departing thunder of the herd of ghost dinosaurs, he and Stevie nodded to each other.

"A jet taking off," Mr. Keegan said.

"No," said Danny. He hurriedly told them what he'd seen. As he spoke, Gramps investigated the wall through which the ghost dinosaurs had come.

"Just a nightmare," Mrs. Keegan said. She came over and sat on the bed between the boys and put her arms around their shoulders. She made him fell better, but Danny wished she wouldn't do that kind of stuff while people were watching.

Stevie said, "But we weren't asleep. And we *both* saw them."

Barbara stood in the doorway rubbing her eyes. She was wearing pink pajamas with feet. She said, "What's the matter?" and yawned.

"Did you see anything funny in your room just now?" Danny said.

"Funny?"

Mrs. Keegan poked Danny in the back with one finger and said, "Danny thought he heard a noise."

19

Danny caught on to what his mom was doing. If Barbara hadn't noticed the ghost dinosaurs, she obviously hadn't seen them. There was no point frightening her. For one thing, if she was scared nobody would get any sleep that night.

"Probably Stevie's brain working," Barbara said, and shuffled away, eyes half closed.

Mrs. Keegan stood up and said, "Barbara has the right idea. Whatever you think happened, it wasn't real. Forget about it and go to sleep."

"What do you say, Gramps?" Danny said.

Gramps kept looking at the wall through which the ghost dinosaurs had come. As if dreaming himself, he said, "I heard about ghost dinosaurs once." He shook his head and said in a normal voice, "but that was a long time ago."

"Stop kidding him, Dad," Mr. Keegan said. "You boys go to sleep. If you feel the need, we can talk more about ghost dinosaurs in the morning." He pushed Gramps out. Mrs. Keegan waved to them and went out, closing the door.

Stevie said, "You better not try that again."

"Try what?"

"To drive me crazy. I'm staying whether you like it or not."

"Stevie, if you think *I* made those ghost dinosaurs, you're already crazy."

Danny went to bed and turned out the light. He lay in the dark listening to Stevie fidget in his sleeping bag. Danny decided that the next day they would take the Eye of Brooklyn to the Brooklyn Museum of Natural History and see what the experts knew about it.

The next morning, Mrs. Keegan took Barbara to ballet class while Mr. Keegan and Gramps went to the hardware store to pick up some nails and screws for a little home improvement project Mr. Keegan had been saving for his father's arrival.

"You want to go to the Brooklyn Museum of Natural History?" Danny asked as he pulled on his shoes. "They have a lot of old stuff on display. Maybe somebody there knows something about the Eye of Brooklyn."

Stevie looked up from a comic book and said, "You mean that piece of glass?"

"A piece of glass couldn't have made those dinosaurs run through my room last night."

"Maybe it was the green beans," Stevie said and laughed.

Not long after that Elisa arrived with Howie Wolfner. Howie was not as tall as the Stein kids, but he was very good at sports. He had long reddish brown hair that came to a point between his eyes. During thunderstorms and when he wanted to, he could turn into a wolf. At the moment, he was carrying a skateboard, and a pair of earphones hung around his neck. The earphones were connected by a skinny wire to a yellow box on his belt.

"Tally ho, chums," he said and looked around warily.

"It's OK to come in," said Danny, "Harryhausen's playing in the backyard."

"Good show," Howie said and followed Elisa inside.

Danny could appreciate Howie's problem. Because he was a werewolf, Howie made dogs and cats feel very uncomfortable. Harryhausen, Danny's beagle, was scared of Howie even though Howie had never done more than look at him. Howie generally liked to avoid dogs and cats when he could.

"New radio?" Danny asked and tapped the yellow box.

"No such thing, old man. It plays cassette tapes. I listen to music while I skateboard. Good for the rhythm, you know. Hello, Stevie. What are you doing here?"

"He just showed up," Danny said.

"You invited me," said Stevie angrily.

Howie looked from one of them to the other and said, "I see. Perhaps you would care to explain that when you have the chance."

"We'll have plenty of time," Danny said. "We're going to the Brooklyn Museum of Natural History. Want to come?"

"Jolly good."

Elisa explained that Frankie would not be joining them. "He is working on something. Electronic parts are everywhere in his lab."

"I hope whatever it is takes pictures of ghosts," Stevie said. After that, Danny and Stevie had to explain what had happened the night before.

"Extraordinary," Howie said. "I can see why you want to visit the museum."

"You believe us?" Danny asked.

"Belief is perhaps too strong a word," Howie said, "but any event on which you and Stevie agree is worth looking into."

The dinosaur statue was too heavy to carry all the way to the museum, but Danny carried the Eye in his pocket. The day was beautiful and the walk to the museum was pleasant. Danny told the story of Stevie's arrival from his point of view, and then Stevie told his version.

Howie said, "It's a bloomin' mystery, all right. What do you say, Elisa?"

"Perhaps it means nothing. But Stevie's arrival immediately followed the Eye of Brooklyn falling out of the statue."

"Meaning what?" said Stevie.

"Perhaps it is only an interesting coincidence."

They walked by what looked like a large lake. It was surrounded by a chain link fence, and a small grassy island rose from the middle of it like a wart. Danny knew it wasn't really a lake but a bog known only as the Bog. The land was soft and squishy and would not support buildings. Danny had heard that draining it was impossible. He imagined that it had changed little since prehistoric times, even after people settled in Brooklyn.

He'd been warned away from the place often enough. Sometimes birds or small animals were caught in it. Once, the body of an escaped convict had been found.

The kids stopped to watch the light wind ripple the bog's surface.

"Look," said Elisa. "Clumps show above the water."

"Huh," Danny acknowledged. "I never saw that before. There are some flowers too."

Howie said, "By Jove, I think the water level is lower than it used to be."

Stevie threw a rock into the bog and they watched it sink. Bubbles came from the place where it went down.

"Well, *that* was boring," Stevie said.

"If we let it, nature can teach us many lessons," Elisa said as they walked on.

"I get all the lessons I need in school," Stevie said. "And they're boring too."

The Brooklyn Museum of Natural History was a big stone building with hundreds of windows and tall Greek columns all around the outside walls. Steps extended across the entire front of the building. In the triangular part below the roof, statues of people without many clothes on were measuring stuff and shining light through lenses and dissecting frogs.

The kids walked up the wide steps and into the cool building. As he walked through the door, Danny noticed something in his pocket getting warm. Even before he took it out, he knew the warm thing was the Eye of Brooklyn.

"Look at this, guys," he said. He let the Eye rest in the palm of his hand, not only warm but glowing in the dim room. Everyone was impressed. Even Stevie said, "Maybe it isn't just a marble."

"Yes," said Elisa. "An oddity such as this should get us in to see the experts."

A guard told them where to go, and they walked through the crowded exhibits. They saw rooms furnished as they had been in different centuries, and stuffed animals set up in lifelike dioramas. On the other side of the Animals of North America gallery they found a room in which the skeletons of dinosaurs, big as steam shovels, bristling with teeth and claws, caught the air in their enormous rib cages. A few other people were there, mostly adults with little kids.

"What a treasure trove for some dog," Howie said.

While they stood at the chain barrier around the skeleton of a stegosaurus, marveling at the armor plates on his back, they heard a loud creaking sound. Everyone turned to look.

Elisa said, "I am having what are known as *the creeps*."

Danny said, "Wasn't that tyrannosaurus looking the other way before?"

Chapter Three

Chances Are

"I swear, Keegan," said Stevie, "if you're trying to scare me again—"

"He's doing a ripping good job of it, I'd say," Howie said.

The neck bones of the tyrannosaurus creaked as he lowered his head to look down at them. Danny began to quiver and sweat as he and the others backed away. They were too frightened even to shriek. Creaking began all around them as other dinosaur skeletons awoke.

A man with a small child looked at the moving skeletons calmly and said, "This is an amazing exhibit, isn't it, Charlie?"

Charlie, evidently much smarter than his dad, began to cry, and the man hurriedly took him away. Others left too and soon Danny, Howie, Elisa, and Stevie were alone with the dinosaurs.

Danny held the Eye of Brooklyn in the palm of his

hand. It was definitely glowing much brighter than before. And it felt warmer.

"OK, Keegan," said Stevie. "I'm convinced. It's not just a marble. Turn it off."

"I don't know how," Danny said through gritted teeth.

The tyrannosaurus creaked more as he stepped delicately over the chain barrier. The triceratops, sort of a rhinocerous with three horns and a high bone collar, broke his chain with one horn and wandered into the next gallery, where Danny heard terrified shouts. The stegosaurus seemed confused as he blundered right through the chain around him, but the tyrannosaurus followed Danny, Howie, Elisa, and Stevie with its head and then began to stalk them.

Guards ran into the room, some with pistols drawn. Danny doubted the weapons would be of any use. "You kids get out of here," one of the guards cried while he watched the tyrannosaurus.

"We are just leaving," said Elisa loudly. She whispered to Danny, "We must take the Eye away."

They ran from the room and Danny heard pistol shots, sounding like somebody breaking pencils next to his ear. He could not help himself. When he was at the far end of the Animals of North America gallery, he turned to look back through the big doorway at the opposite end and saw the tyrannosaurus slowing until it froze in midstride. The museum was very quiet now that the creaking had stopped.

"Let's go," Stevie said.

"Right-o, then," said Howie. "For once I'm with Stevie."

By the most direct route, they hurried through the exhibits and out of the museum. They ran down the steps and clustered on the sidewalk facing the building. The Eye of Brooklyn no longer glowed or felt warm. They all laughed, but it was the nervous laughter of relief.

Howie looked back at the museum and said, "I wouldn't be those guard blokes for anything."

"Yes," said Elisa. "They will have some difficulty explaining why the skeletons are not in their accustomed places."

"I'm having a little problem with that myself," Stevie Brickwald said.

They all stared at Danny. He said, "Now do you believe us about the ghost dinosaurs?"

Howie and Elisa nodded.

"You know," said Danny as he began to walk home, "I think the Brooklyn Museum of Natural History was the wrong place to come for information."

"Indeed," said Howie. "Perhaps Zelda Bella would be more helpful."

Zelda Bella was a Gypsy they knew. She was not only the host of *Mother Scary's Matinee,* but she was a real witch. She frequently knew things that other adults could not even guess.

"I'd like to talk to my grandfather first," said Danny. "Sort of keep it in the family."

"Keep what?" Stevie said.

"I don't know; whatever this is," Danny said and shook his head.

They walked for a while in silence. Howie said, "If you ask me, I'd say that bauble has a curse on it."

"What's a bauble?" Stevie asked.

"In this case it's the Eye of Brooklyn," said Howie.

Already uncomfortable, Danny asked, "What do you mean by *curse*?"

"Look at the evidence," Howie said. "First Stevie shows up at your house."

Stevie shoved his fist under Howie's nose and said, "I ain't no curse, dog breath."

Howie was unimpressed. He said, "Take that away or I will howl at you."

Stevie kept the fist up for a second and then let it drop. Like the rest of them, Stevie had heard Howie's howl. It was frightening, like something wild that was heard but unseen, even when you knew it was only Howie making the noise. Stevie said again, "I ain't no curse."

"That remains a matter of opinion," Howie said. "Then there is the matter of the stampede of the ghost dinosaurs. Certainly not favorable conditions for a good night's sleep."

"You got that right," Stevie said.

"Then the attack of the tyrannosaurus skeleton. And then there's the matter of the draining bog."

"I can see how that dinosaur stuff might be caused by a curse," Danny said, "and not even Stevie knows exactly how he got to my house." Stevie shook his head and Danny went on, "But how is the bog draining bad luck? And for whom?"

Elisa said, "I believe neither in curses nor in luck."

"What do you believe in?" Danny asked.

They walked for a while before Elisa answered, "I believe in probability shifts."

"I was just gonna say that," Stevie said and laughed.

Elisa said, "There is a low but real chance that the molecules in those dinosaur bones would move in such a way that the skeletons would seem to be alive. Just as there is a low but real chance that all the air in a room will compress itself into one corner."

"There is?" Stevie asked fearfully.

"Yes, but the chances are very low indeed. You are more likely to be killed by a falling meteor."

While they glanced suspiciously at the sky, Elisa went on, "I think the probability shift was caused by an imbalance. I believe that returning the Eye of Brooklyn to the socket in the stone dinosaur will correct the imbalance."

By this time the three boys were staring at Elisa with mild amazement. Howie said, "Blimy, Elisa, that's the kind of stuff I expect to hear from Frankie."

Elisa smiled and said, "You must give me some credit. I have not been Frankie's sister for all these years without learning something of science."

"Look at that," said Danny.

They had come to the bog again, only something new had been added, and Danny was pointing to it.

Just inside the chain link fence, a big wooden sign had been planted in the solid ground that the receding waters had revealed. The sign said COMING SOON! BEAUTIFUL DINOSAUR BOG ESTATES! And then in smaller letters, *Another Tasteful Rogers and Fishman Development*.

"Crikey!" said Howie. "It seems the bog had a name after all."

"More dinosaurs," said Danny. "I hope Dad and Gramps are back from the hardware store. I have to talk to Gramps right now." He began to run.

Chapter Four

Ancient Keegan History

"They're here," Danny cried, and ran into the house. "Dad! Gramps!" To Stevie and his friends he said, "You guys go up to the attic and see if you can find anything else in that trunk."

"Jolly good," said Howie and led the way upstairs.

Danny searched the house, which was empty, and at last found his dad and Gramps in the garage puzzling over some boards they'd laid out on the cement floor.

"Gramps, I have to talk to you."

"Hang on a minute, young feller. Your father and I have about figured out how this bookcase is going together."

"This is important."

"Don't whine, Danny," Mr. Keegan said without looking up.

Danny stood on one foot and then the other while the two men moved the boards around. At last they had the boards in a satisfactory pattern and Gramps said, "All right, Danny. I think I can trust your father to start screwing this sucker together. What's your problem?''

Mr. Keegan was so engrossed in his bookcase that he didn't even notice Danny dragging Gramps away. When they were at the other end of the driveway, Danny said, "Is the Eye of Brooklyn cursed?"

Gramps looked at Danny with a small smile on his face. He said, "You just leap right in, don't you, boy?"

"I guess so, sir. Is it?"

"What makes you ask?"

Danny sighed. Telling an adult the kind of story he had in mind was always a chancy business. Some adults pretended they hadn't heard you. Others pretended they'd heard something else, or tried to cram the strange events into their everyday world. Sometimes adults just got angry and told you not to be silly.

"Spit it out, boy," Gramps said. "You look as if you've just swallowed a pinch bug."

"Yes, sir." Danny decided to tell Gramps everything. He had a feeling that Gramps would understand. Gramps already knew about Stevie's arrival, but hadn't yet connected it with the Eye of Brooklyn. Danny reminded him about the ghost dinosaurs and then related how the skeletons at the museum had stomped around. "And then there's Dinosaur Bog," Danny said.

Gramps listened to Danny with no more and no less concentration than he'd given to Barbara's blathering about ballet the day before. He nodded in all the right places and even asked a few questions. Now he said, "What about Dinosaur Bog?"

"You know it?"

"Of course. It's been the same since even I can remember."

"Has it always been called Dinosaur Bog?"

"Sure. By those in the know. What about it?"

"It's draining all by itself and somebody's going to build houses on it."

"Hmm," said Gramps and frowned.

"So," said Danny, "is the Eye of Brooklyn cursed? And if it is, how do we stop it?"

Gramps got that faraway look in his eye again and he didn't say anything for a long time. Danny was eager to hear an answer, but he thought he might get a better one if he didn't rush Gramps.

Gramps said, "Everything's going to be all right."

"You know how to lift the curse?"

"I didn't say that. I said everything's going to be all right."

"What does *that* mean?" Danny asked.

Gramps shook his head and said, "You'll have to trust me. It all happened such a long time ago. I hardly remember the details."

"All what happened? What details?" This was very frustrating.

Gramps squeezed Danny's shoulder and said, "Trust me," again. As he strolled toward the garage, he said, "I have to go supervise your father before he makes too big a mess of that bookcase."

Standing there at the end of the driveway, Danny felt abandoned. Did Gramps really know anything or was he just afraid to admit to a kid that he knew nothing? But if he did know something why was he so secretive about it? Gramps didn't seem to be the type who would tell a kid, "You'll understand when you're older."

Danny went into the house and then up to the attic. Howie and Elisa were flipping through magazines while sitting on others that had been tied in stacks. Stevie was leaping around the attic making fantastic imaginary saves with the broken tennis racket.

When Danny entered they all stopped what they were doing and looked at him. Elisa said, "What does your grandfather say?"

"His exact words were 'Trust me.' "

"Dash it all, he said nothing else?" Howie asked.

"He said he's having trouble remembering things that happened a long time ago."

Stevie lobbed the tennis racket into a corner where it crashed against an old bird cage. He said, "Sounds as if your old gramps has lost his grip."

Elisa said, "Even if this is true, it is not polite to say so."

Stevie shrugged and said, "Sometimes the truth hurts."

Though Danny feared that Stevie was right, he didn't feel like discussing it. He said, "Let's take a look in the trunk. Maybe we'll find a clue or something."

Danny, Howie, and Elisa got on their knees in front of the trunk in which they'd found the dinosaur statue. Stevie stood over them heckling. In the trunk they found some old clothes, a 1930 *Boy Scout Manual*, dishes, and a wind-up clock that rattled when Danny shook it.

"Hey, look at this," Danny said. He picked up an oblong of cardboard that was lying facedown on the bottom of the trunk. He turned it over and saw that it was a photograph in a gray cardboard frame.

The picture was old and brown but it clearly showed two people, each wearing a flat cap. A man no older than Danny's father had his arm around the shoulder of a boy about Danny's age. Neither of them was smiling. Both wore suits and ties in a style that Danny had never seen worn outside a movie. The coats had short heavy lapels, and were buttoned tight, as if they were a half size too small.

"Blimy," said Howie, "the oldest people I know don't dress like that."

"Yeah," said Danny. "Gramps always dresses as if he's going to play golf."

"Who are they?" Elisa said.

Gently, Danny turned the picture over and saw writing that was so faded he'd missed it before. It was done in bold flourishes, like the writing in the Declaration of Independence. Out loud, Danny read, "Mr. Thadeus Keegan and his son, David." He took a deep breath and said, "Gosh! The kid in this picture is Gramps."

Danny was amazed. He knew that Gramps had been young once. Everybody who got old had been young once. Yet knowing it and believing it were two different things. Danny shook his head as he stared at the picture, feeling the great gulf of time that separated him from the kid in the picture, that separated Gramps himself from the kid in the picture. The gulf felt like the Grand Canyon.

"There is a family resemblance," Elisa said.

Stevie said, "What a snore. You guys can stand here

and discuss ancient Keegan history if you want. I'm going to find a comic book." He strolled off.

Danny barely heard Stevie. He continued to stare at the photograph. He could not stop saying, "Amazing," over and over again. It was probably his imagination, but in his pocket, the Eye of Brooklyn seemed to be warming up again. The photo grew larger and larger, and soon it filled Danny's entire universe. Every second Thadeus and David Keegan seemed about to move.

Danny grew dizzy for a moment and he closed his eyes. When he opened them he blinked. The scene in front of him was the same as it had been before his dizzy spell. But before it had been a photograph. Now it was real!

Chapter Five

All in Color

A man said, "Hold it," and Danny froze, certain that he had been caught and not knowing what, if anything, he ought to do about it. Standing behind the man, Danny saw only that he wore a loose white shirt and wide gray pants held up by suspenders. His hair was red and curly.

The man who had spoken ducked under a black cloth and looked through a big camera on a tripod. He held aloft a narrow tray on a stick. The stuff in the tray exploded and gave off a bright light, like a flash of lightning. "All right," the man said.

David and Thadeus Keegan had been sitting stiffly, and now they moved normally, kind of shaking themselves out. When David stood up, Danny saw that his pants came down just below his knee. The space between the pants and the shoes was taken up by gray socks.

Thadeus stared at Danny and his friends and said with some surprise, "Who are you?"

37

The photographer turned around and looked at Danny, Howie, and Elisa, even more surprised than Thadeus. He had large fleshy features and a big red mustache that curled up at the ends. He said, "If you three want a photograph, you'll have to make an appointment." He peered at them as if through smoke and went on, "Say, you're not from around here are you?"

"Aren't we?" said Howie. He and Elisa looked at Danny.

Danny was aware that something very strange had happened. Once, a machine built by Frankie Stein had carried him to a parallel universe, a place almost exactly like the Brooklyn he knew but with interesting differences. Danny was certain that he'd traveled a lot farther this time. He, Howie, and Elisa were still in the right Brooklyn, but together the Eye and the photograph had transported them back in time to when Gramps was a child!

He was also aware of how conspicuous they looked. None of them was dressed for the trip, all three of them wearing jeans and T-shirts. Howie's said BORN TO HOWL on the front. Elisa also had on a pair of peacock blue leg warmers that Barbara had allowed her to borrow. The chest of Danny's shirt had a picture of Bugs Bunny on it.

Danny thought about the story he would have to invent for the benefit of David and Thadeus and the photographer. Danny and his friends had to be from someplace far away, and yet not too far away to be believed. Danny said, "No, we're not from around here. We're from California." He was glad he hadn't said, We just flew in from California.

"I can believe that," Thadeus said. "I hear they do things different on the western coast." He and the boy and the photographer laughed.

"Where are you staying?" David asked.

"Staying?" Danny said.

Elisa said, "We have not yet decided."

Danny instantly knew that Elisa had made a mistake saying that. Kids their age didn't just cross the country by themselves unless relatives or good friends were waiting for them.

Thadeus said, "You'd best come with us." He handed the photographer a coin and went out with David. Danny, Howie, and Elisa followed the two down a long narrow stairway to the street.

Danny and his friends stood gaping in front of the photographer's door. Big horses pulling wagons were mixed in with old black automobiles that putted by as if powered by lawn mower engines—although at the moment, these automobiles were probably no older than the ones Danny saw every day. The smell of horse-leavings and of automobile exhaust was intense.

Though the air was not cold, everybody wore a hat. The men wore dark suits and the woman long heavy dresses containing yards and yards of cloth. Compared with modern Brooklyn, this version was mostly empty space. Between two square ten-story buildings made of brick might be a small farm complete with chickens and goats.

But the most astonishing thing about this earlier Brooklyn had nothing to do with space or the presence of horses or even the fact of time travel itself. Howie whispered to Danny, "It's all in color!"

"Of course," Elisa said.

It was all very well for Elisa to remain cool, but Danny had been thinking exactly the same thing. After all, history lived for him mainly through TV, movies, and books. Most pictures he'd seen of eras before he was born—moving or still—had been in black and white. He knew that the world had always been in color, just as he knew Gramps had once been a little boy. He just had trouble believing it.

David must have noticed their surprise. He said, "I guess you don't have cities this big in California."

"It's real different," Danny agreed. He put his hands into his pockets and stiffened.

"What's the matter?" David said.

"Uh, nothing," Danny said. "Just overcome by the size of the city." He let David walk ahead with his father. When Danny was more or less alone with Howie and Elisa, he said, "We have a problem. I can't find the Eye."

"You didn't bring it with you?" Howie asked, astonished.

"I was holding it when we left, but I guess not."

"Very interesting," Elisa said.

"Very disastrous," Howie said.

Danny wondered if he would like living in a time before he was born. He said, "What are we going to do?"

"Perhaps something will present itself," Elisa said.

"Something like what?" Danny and Howie said together.

"Don't dawdle, children," Thadeus said as he walked down the street.

41

As Danny and his friends ran to catch up, Danny tried to enjoy being where he was. Elisa was right. Something would present itself. And if it didn't, well this time wasn't so bad. He'd always liked horses.

Though this Brooklyn was a little light on buildings, people were everywhere. They clotted in clumps at the curb holding discussions and loud arguments, frequently in languages that Danny was not familiar with. Every street corner had a news vendor or a guy selling bagels or *something*.

Girls jumped rope and boys played a game that looked a lot like baseball but was played using broomsticks or whatever else was at hand. The girls were dressed in long dresses and more often than not, their hair was in pigtails. The boys had their uniform too, much like the outfit David was wearing, only occasionally without the jacket. They kept their pants up with suspenders.

Danny and Howie attracted attention, but Elisa was the greater source of interest. Evidently, girls wearing pants were so rare as to be unknown. "Many girls in California wear pants?" Thadeus asked.

"Some," said Elisa.

David and his father enjoyed watching them, and through them were entertained all over again by their own city. Neither Danny nor Howie nor Elisa corrected their assumption that the three new kids were hicks from some uncivilized part of California.

One group of boys actually stopped playing their game when Danny and the others walked by and gaped as if Danny and his friends were from outer space. Danny wondered how kids in his own time would have reacted if kids dressed in knee pants, coats, and flat caps just dropped out of the sky one day.

Thadeus said, "You children can stay and play if you'd like. I have work to do."

"What do you say?" David asked Danny, Howie, and Elisa.

"Sure," said Danny. "I'm always up for a game."

"Good show," said Howie enthusiastically.

When Mr. Thadeus Keegan walked away, the largest of the boys started to laugh, and the others followed his lead.

"Ain't they the cat's pajamas?" a smaller boy next to him said.

The big boy laughed again and slapped his hands against his legs. He said, "Looks to me as if they're *wearing* the cat's pajamas."

The smaller boy, obviously the leader's chief admirer, made a single loud "Haw!" and then the two groups just stared at each other.

Something about the big kid kind of reminded Danny of Stevie Brickwald. Evidently no era was without its bullies.

"By Jove," said Howie, "what cheek that bloke has!"

"He sure talks pretty, don't he, boys?" the big kid asked in a way that suggested he already had the answer he wanted. "Hello, Dave," he said. "I see you prefer the company of foreigners to that of native Americans."

Just loud enough for Danny, Howie, and Elisa to hear, David said, "A foreigner is somebody who's been in the United States less than a week. Anybody who's

been here more than a month generally considers himself a native.''

"Who is this offensive person?'' Elisa asked.

"That's Jacob's cousin Theodore.''

"Poor Jacob,'' Danny said.

"Yeah,'' said David. "Theodore Brickwald arrived on Jacob's family's front stoop one morning with no more explanation than a stray cat.''

"Theodore *Brickwald*?'' Danny asked in surprise.

"You know the Brickwalds?'' David said.

Danny and his friends glanced at each other. Theodore Brickwald's sudden appearance on Jacob's stoop and here in the middle of their adventure possibly meant nothing. A curse was not responsible every time an unpleasant person made a surprise visit.

Elisa said, "We have Brickwalds in California.''

Howie said, "I believe that I will teach this particular Brickwald some manners.''

As Howie strode forward, David said worriedly, "Theodore's a hard character. Your friend may need some help.''

"Perhaps not,'' Elisa said. "Watch.''

Howie spoke briefly with Theodore, who laughed and mockingly bowed. Howie went up to where the batter normally stood and hefted the length of broom handle the kids were using for a bat. Theodore snatched the ball off the ground, wound up, and pitched. It was a hard fast one, but Howie got a good piece of it and hit the ball with a loud crack.

All the kids watched as the ball arced high and far and descended behind a building across the street that said EMPORIUM above its big front windows. Many in

Theodore's group whistled or made other noises of appreciation.

Theodore said, "Well, can you beat that?" He swaggered to where Howie was standing and confronted him.

"I believe," said Howie, "that answers any questions you may have about foreigners."

Theodore showed his fist to Howie much as *Stevie* Brickwald might have done. And as he always was with Stevie, Howie remained unimpressed. He threw back his head and howled.

Danny had heard Howie howl before, and in fact had been expecting him to howl now. A werewolf howl had proven to be one of the few successful ways to deal with Stevie Brickwald. Even so, when Howie started, Danny felt cold and frightened. The short hairs on the back of his neck stood up.

The howl had an even stronger effect on the local kids. They backed away from Howie, fingers in their ears. Theodore tried to tough out the situation by just standing there. But the expression on his face became increasingly horrified. His eyes grew wide, and after a few seconds he put his fingers into his ears and backed off like everybody else.

Howie rejoined Danny, Elisa, and David. He dusted off his hands and said, "We can move on now, chums, if it's all the same to you."

David looked at Howie strangely and said, "That was really something. Can you teach me how to do it?"

"Regrettably not, old boy. I'm afraid it's a talent one must be born with."

David nodded and said, "Too bad. Anything that'll dust Theodore is worth learning."

They passed the bog and Danny stopped.

"Never seen a bog before?" David asked, amused.

"Uh, no," Howie said. "Dry as dust in California, you know."

As Gramps had said, the bog was much the same in this earlier time as it would be/had been in the future. (Danny saw that if time travel became common, an entire new set of tenses would be needed.) The only difference he could see was that no one had yet put up a fence around it.

"Look," said David, "somebody put up a sign."

They strolled around the bog until they could read the sign. It said: INCOMPARABLE HOMES AT LOW PRICES WILL SOON BE BUILT HERE ON DINOSAUR BOG.

"The bog must be draining here too," Elisa said.

David said, "I thought you didn't have bogs in California."

"We have visited many places," Elisa said. "Some of them have bogs that drain." Once again, Elisa had managed to evade a question without quite telling a lie.

David nodded, but he didn't seem to be convinced.

Danny said, "Dinosaur Bog. Interesting name. Are there many dinosaurs around here?"

"Not many," David said and laughed. "Do you have dinosaurs in California?"

"No," said Elisa firmly.

Howie looked at Elisa, shrugged, and said, "No."

Danny just shook his head and said, "What do you mean 'not many'?"

David sat down on the low cement wall around a park, and the others joined him. He said, "I don't know if I should tell you."

47

"Why not?" said Danny.

"It's very strange," said David. "And it's not my story to tell."

"Toe in and blast away, old man," Howie said.

"What?"

Elisa said, "Tell us. We are most sympathetic to strange events."

"Quite," Howie said.

David nodded as he considered. He chuckled and said, "I guess I owe you something for showing up Theodore."

Danny, Elisa, and Howie chuckled with him, and then waited.

David said, "Remember Jacob?"

"Theodore's unfortunate cousin?" said Howie.

"You hit that nail right on the head. Well, he's been having dinosaur trouble lately. Or at least, that's what he says. I think he's just telling a big story."

David stopped and Danny said, "I don't know about the others, but you have *my* attention."

David said, "He tells me that ghost dinosaurs have been running through his room."

"Ghost dinosaurs?" Danny asked excitedly.

"I told you it was just a big story."

"Please continue," Elisa said.

"That's really all," David said. "A big story, like I said."

"I think it's time we met Jacob," said Danny.

"Sure. If you want to," David said as he stood up. "He's generally in an empty lot near here playing marbles."

Danny thought about the Eye of Brooklyn and how much it looked like a marble. Maybe Elisa's prediction was coming true already. Something was about to present itself.

Chapter Six

Losing Your Marbles

Walking through this old Brooklyn was like walking through an amusement park. Everywhere Danny looked he saw things he'd never seen before outside the movies. People looked at him and Howie and Elisa, but none of them went so far as to make fun of them, as Theodore had.

The empty lot David had spoken of was not far away. And it was less a lot than it was a weedy field. In one corner of it an open space about the size of Danny's room at home had been cleared, and in the center of the open space some boys were on their knees around a circle gouged into the dirt.

"Come on, Stanley," cried a skinny boy. "Are you going to shoot or aren't you?"

"I'm lining up my shot," Stanley said, whining. His back end rose and fell as he set his cheek against the ground and sighted behind a big clear marble with a green swirl inside. Then he flicked the big clear marble with his thumb and it shot, as if from a gun, into the mass of marbles scattered near the middle of the circle. The big marble knocked the others around, and two of them were knocked out of the circle—a very small red one, and one that looked like a planet, a mottled green, blue, and white. Stanley came up off the ground smiling and with a smudge of dirt on his cheek.

The skinny boy groaned as Stanley eagerly picked up the two marbles. He lined up his shooter again, taking his time, and shot, knocking out three more marbles. On his third turn, Stanley banged the marbles around a little, but knocked none of them out of the circle.

The game moved on to the next boy, who had even better luck than Stanley. And each time he knocked a marble out of the circle, the skinny boy groaned.

"There's Jacob," David whispered, "the thin boy who keeps losing."

That made sense to Danny. If Jacob really had the Eye of Brooklyn in his possession, he was probably cursed. Losing at marbles would be part of it, just as Theodore's arrival and the draining bog were part of it.

When Jacob's turn came, he knelt, his head low, his other end high, and sighted along his own shooter, a big clear marble that looked like the Eye of Brooklyn. If Jacob would let Danny borrow it before he lost it, and if Danny could figure out what he'd done before, could it send him and his friends home? Jacob shot and missed the other marbles entirely.

"What's the matter with you, Jake?" one of the boys said. "You used to be the hottest marbles player in the neighborhood."

"Arnie's right," said Stanley. "You better quit before you lose that big glassy shooter of yours too."

Jacob stared morosely at the game till David said, "Jacob?" He looked up, but appeared no happier to see David and the others than he'd been to study the marbles circle.

"Come on, Jacob," David said. "We want to talk to you."

"About what?" Jacob said without interest.

On a hunch, Danny said, "About marbles."

Jacob looked from them to the circle and back again. He collected the few marbles he had left into a small canvas bag and stood up. Without another word, Jacob set out for the other side of the lot.

"Is he balmy or what?" Howie said.

"*Or what*, perhaps," said Elisa.

"I don't know what balmy means, but if it means that Jacob is a strange duck, you're right."

Jacob led them down the street at the far side of the lot and into another lot; then he entered what appeared to be an old tumbledown barn. Inside, the stalls leaned crazily and the straw—of which there was plenty—was old and dirty. The air smelled thick and damp.

Jacob stopped in the middle of the barn and said, "What do you want?" He shocked Danny when he took a homemade cigarette from his jacket pocket and lit it with a match that he struck on the bottom of his shoe. As he puffed, Elisa said, "Smoking will make you sick and then it will kill you."

"Sez you," said Jacob.

Here was another instance in which Danny was surprised by actually seeing something despite the fact he'd

52

heard about it before. He'd known for a long time that people used to smoke without thinking much about how it polluted their lungs. Even kids in books sometimes smoked—Huckleberry Finn, for instance, smoked a pipe. But seeing a kid smoke right in front of him, smelling the fumes, was astonishing.

"Can't you be good?" David said. "These are my friends. They're from California."

"Sez them," Jacob said. "What do they want?"

"Can I see your shooter?" Danny asked.

"Why?" said Jacob.

Danny wondered how much they could safely tell Jacob. They'd managed to get by without telling David much of anything, but Jacob seemed like a much harder case. Evidently David mistook Danny's thoughtful silence for shyness because he said, "I told them about the ghost dinosaurs."

"That wasn't smart," Jacob said and puffed angrily on his cigarette.

"It's OK," Danny said as he waved away the irritating smoke. "Really. I've seen them too."

The smoke continued to rise, but everything else stopped as David and Jacob stared at him. "You're kidding," David said.

"You don't have to baby me," Jacob said. He threw the cigarette onto the floor, crushed it out with his heel, and strode toward the opening between the two sagging doors.

"Really," called Danny. Jacob stopped and Danny went on, "I've also had a terrible visitor drop in unexpectedly." Jacob turned around. Danny said, "I think all this has something to do with that shooter you're using. I don't think it's really a marble."

"What is it?" David and Jacob said together.

"It's the Eye of Brooklyn."

"The what?"

"They Eye of Brooklyn. I don't understand everything myself, but if you remove the Eye from the socket in the dinosaur statue it comes in, it puts a curse on whoever owns it, and it drains Dinosaur Bog."

"It is not a curse," said Elisa. "It is a shift in the probability curve."

"What did she say?" David said.

"Dash it all," cried Howie. "What she said doesn't matter. What matters is lifting the curse, if that's what it is."

"Yeah," said Danny. "Neither one of us wants our guest to stay forever."

Elisa said, "And perhaps if the Eye were returned, you would occasionally win at marbles."

Elisa's argument made Jacob think. "I didn't tell anybody about the dinosaur statue," he said quietly. "Not even big mouth over there."

"I told you," said Danny. "I have a statue too."

"Maybe you do and maybe you don't. What do you want?"

"I thought that was obvious, old man," Howie said. "We want to return the Eye to its socket."

We want to send us home, Danny thought.

"I tried it," Jacob said. "I can't make it go."

"Me too," said Danny. "Maybe we can work on it together."

Jacob said, "Maybe," but he was also nodding,

which led Danny to believe that they'd managed to convince him at last.

"Come on," said Jacob. "I'll take you to my secret place."

Chapter Seven

Jacob's Secret Place

Jacob led them through Brooklyn. They went around corners, across fields, and in at the front door of a butcher shop. It was a real butcher shop with sawdust on the floor and real butchers in white aprons; nothing was wrapped in plastic. They followed Jacob out the back, down alleys, through parks, and over fences. He seemed surprised that Elisa was able to keep up. He would not have been surprised if he'd known her better.

Because he was unfamiliar with the Brooklyn of this time, Danny could not be sure, but he got the impression that Jacob was trying to confuse them by taking the long way around. Maybe he wanted to make certain that they would not be able to find his secret place without his help. As it turned out, he was more likely just entertaining himself or showing off because the place to which he took them was unmistakable. Any of them would be able to find it again, no matter what time they came from.

They stood at one edge of Dinosaur Bog looking out at the island in the center. Behind them was an office building with a restaurant on the ground floor.

"I have bad news for you, old boy," Howie said. "This place is not secret."

"A wise guy," Jacob said sarcastically. "Come on." He took his bearings from a lamppost and stepped carefully into the bog.

None of the passersby seemed to care or even to notice what Jacob was doing, but Elisa cried out, "Do not go out there. Surely, you will drown."

"Another wise guy. Are you coming or aren't you? If you are, put your feet exactly where I put mine or you *will* drown."

With his usual daring, Howie leaped after Jacob. The others followed with less enthusiasm. David was the last. From the bog came a terrible smell of decaying vegetation and of water that had been standing too long in one place. The smell was so bad it was just as well that Jacob's pace was brisk.

He had obviously made this journey many times before. Danny followed exactly in Elisa's footsteps as she followed in Howie's. They all had to move pretty fast not only to keep up with Jacob, but also because water quickly seeped into footprints, obliterating them, and no one wanted to be trapped on a firm place in the middle of the bog, not knowing where to step next.

With some relief, Danny walked up the gradually sloping bank of solid ground that circled the island. He sat down on a big rock and looked around. If Danny was any judge of the curve of the island's shoreline, he could probably walk around the whole thing in less than half an hour. Wild grass grew among the rocks and in places made a waving green sea that came up to Danny's waist. The few tall thin trees shuddered in the foul wind that blew off the bog. In the middle of the island was a jumbled mound of house-sized boulders.

Jacob looked around proudly and said, "Nobody bothers me here."

"I'll bet," Danny said.

Jacob appraised him, as if Danny had said something insulting and Jacob were deciding whether to take offense. Jacob said, "This is my biggest secret. Nobody else knows how to get over here, and it took over a year for *me* to figure out how."

"Ripping," said Howie. "Most impressive."

"Nertz to that kind of talk," Jacob said. "The point is that I showed you my big secret. Now you have to tell me yours."

Suddenly wary, Danny said, "What secret?"

"You have to tell me where you're from."

"Not California?" David said.

"I'd be very surprised," Jacob said.

Danny said, "Wait a minute," and walked down the beach to huddle with his friends. "Should we tell them?" he asked.

Elisa said, "Influencing the past is always dangerous. If we tell them anything they would not have known otherwise, the future we came from may no longer exist. We may find it impossible to go home."

Danny shrugged and said, "Unless Jacob's shooter is the Eye of Brooklyn, we may not be able to get home anyway. And even if it is, it may be the *wrong* Eye. Too old or too new." Danny shrugged again. "Or

58

something. I'm pretty vague about how all this works."
They stared at each other for a while, each thinking
private thoughts about Danny's statement. Jacob and
David threw pebbles into the bog, making bull's-eyes
in targets of ripples.

"Crikey, Danny's right," said Howie. "And even
if we have the proper Eye, we certainly don't have a
photograph of Danny's attic to concentrate on."

"Something," said Elisa, "will present itself. It may
already have. But if worse comes to worst, we will
travel into the future along with everyone else and arrive
as old people."

Growing old many years before he was born was a
solution of sorts and better than being stuck where they
were. Then Danny had a thought that made him smile.
"You know," he said, "if we did arrive in the future
as old people, we would probably go see ourselves as
kids long before Gramps helped us clean out the attic.
Since no old people like that ever visited *us,* that means
we got out of this some way and got home while we
were still kids."

"Perhaps," said Elisa. "Perhaps the wisdom of old
age would tell us not to try visiting ourselves as
children."

Jacob called to them, "Come on, fellows. Put up or
shut up."

"Perhaps," said Howie, "we are safe telling them
anything. Remember, this is the past. Everything has
already happened. Perhaps anything we tell them is part
of the natural flow, part of *our* past as it already was.
Er, is. You know what I mean."

Danny knew what Howie meant: thinking about the

ins and outs of time travel was making his head hurt. He said, "Perhaps. Maybe. Who knows? I think we ought to do what seems right at the moment, and let time take care of itself. I vote we tell them everything."

"Right-o, then, chum," said Howie. "But Jacob must tell us some things first. Allow me to do the talking."

"With pleasure," Elisa said.

Jacob continued to throw pebbles into the bog as they spoke, though David stopped and listened carefully.

Howie said, "We'll tell you all about ourselves if you tell us one more thing."

"What's that?" said Jacob and hurled a stone at the sky. A long moment later it plopped into the bog.

Howie said, "It's bully that you guided us here. Bully. However, I fail to see the connection between this place and the Eye of Brooklyn or the dinosaur statue."

"Yeah," said Danny.

Jacob looked surprised, and then regained his composure. He said, "I guess you're right. Even so, I did show you *a* secret. You owe me one."

Howie's eyebrows went up and he said nothing.

"Go ahead, Howie," Elisa said.

Howie looked at Danny, who nodded.

Howie told Jacob and David everything. About how they weren't really from California, but from the future, from near the end of the twentieth century.

Jacob shook his head and said, "You guys give me a pain. Let's go back." He was walking back toward the bog when Danny said, "Look at this." He held up a slim plastic object.

"What is it?" said Jacob.

"A ballpoint pen."

"A what?" said Jacob and David together.

"I'll show you," he said. He clicked the button at the top and wrote on his hand the word "Brooklyn."

"Where does the ink come from?" David asked.

Danny took the pen apart and passed around the pieces—the two plastic outside parts, the spring, and the refill. Jacob said, "You can't carry much ink in here."

David glanced at the refill and shook his head. He said, "And what is the outside made of? It's not wood or glass or crockery either."

Elisa told them about plastic.

They shook their heads, marveling.

"Listen here, chaps," Howie said. His portable tape player had been clipped to his belt all this time. Danny hadn't noticed it, and evidently nobody else had either. Now Howie switched it on and began to snap his fingers to a band that Danny knew only as the Eruptions.

Jacob and David listened with confusion. If the stuff Danny had found in the trunk in his attic was representative of the music of this time, the rowdy, raucous, driving beat of the music on Howie's tape would be a change of pace for them, if nothing else.

"Where's that noise coming from?" yelled Jacob.

"Right here," Howie yelled back and switched off the player. He popped out the cassette tape cartridge and handed it to Jacob. David watched as he examined it carefully, then held it up to his ear and shook it. "Where do you put the needle down?" Jacob asked.

"No needle," said Howie. "It's all done with magnetism."

Both Jacob and David took a good look inside the compartment where the tape normally went.

Awed, David said, "They didn't buy these things at the local emporium, Jacob. Or in California either."

"No," said Jacob. He handed back the cassette and watched as Howie reloaded his player. "How did you get here?"

Danny said, "We were looking at a photograph of David and his father while I had the Eye of Brooklyn in my pocket, and we just sort of fell in."

"What?" cried Jacob. "Into the picture?"

"That's what seemed to happen."

David looked at Danny with suspicion and said, "What were *you* doing with a picture of me and my father?"

Despite the fact they had decided to tell David and Jacob everything and allow time to take care of itself, Danny was embarrassed by David's question. Maybe his discomfort was caused by the peculiar double vision that came with traveling in time. How would David relate to somebody who was both his grandson and some strange kid about his own age? If Danny was lucky, David would probably not believe a story that appeared to be ridiculous on its face. But if David *did* believe, he would certainly have something new to think about.

Danny smiled in a way that he himself felt was not very sincere, and to blunt the shock, he said in an off-handed way, "I found it in a trunk my parents have

62

had for years. It's a photograph of my grandfather and his father.''

Jacob tried to say something, but David shushed him in such a way that Jacob took the order seriously. Danny could see by the parade of emotions crossing David's face that David was trying to work out what had just been said, see what was in it for him. When the realization struck, David stared at Danny and said slowly, "I'm your grandfather?''

"As far as I can tell.''

"But—'' said David and stopped himself. Danny knew what the problem was. If David was going to buy the time travel story, he felt obligated to buy the grandfather story, and he didn't want to do that.

"I know,'' said Danny. "It gives you a funny feeling right in the pit of your stomach.''

"Yeah,'' David agreed.

"Excuse me,'' said Elisa, "but we are distracted by side issues. Now that we have told Jacob and David *our* secret, it is time for Jacob to tell us how this island is connected with the Eye of Brooklyn.''

Everyone looked at Jacob expectantly.

Jacob said, "You have a lot of ideas for a girl.''

Elisa said, "In the future, this is not unusual.''

"The future must be a strange place.'' He contemplated for a moment and then went on, "Fair is fair. The truth is simple enough.'' He smiled. "Simpler than *your* truth, anyway. I found the Eye here on this island.''

"You removed it from the dinosaur statue?'' Elisa asked.

"Well, yeah," said Jacob, embarrassed. "It's my island. I found the statue. Why not?"

"Now you know why not," Elisa said.

Jacob nodded. "It would be nice if Theodore went home. It would be nice to win at marbles again."

"Ripping!" cried Howie. "Then all we must do is return the Eye to the statue."

"If we can," said Danny. "Remember, I couldn't get the Eye to fit into *my* dinosaur statue, and Jacob couldn't put his back either." He frowned.

"What's the problem, old chum?"

"My Eye of Brooklyn is back in the future where we can't get at it, along with the photograph. Will replacing Jacob's Eye of Brooklyn solve *our* problems? And are they both the same Eye at different times or two different Eyes?"

"Bloomin' complicated, ain't it?" Howie said.

"We have no answers," Elisa said, "but I feel that somehow solving Jacob's problem will help us solve our own." She looked at Jacob and asked, "The dinosaur statue is still on the island?"

"I'll say. It weighs a ton."

"Certainly not a ton," Elisa said. "I suggest you lead us to it immediately."

Without a word, Jacob nodded and set off toward the center of the island. As Danny and the others followed, he said to David, "When you get older, don't buy stocks. During the 1930s there will be a depression."

"What does that mean?"

"I'm not sure, but I know that the stock market crashed and the stocks people had bought were worthless. Lots of people were out of work. Keep your money in one of the big banks and hang on.''

"I don't get it.''

"You will. Just stay awake and remember what I said.''

David shrugged.

Danny was pleased. Chances were good that it was his financial advice that had allowed Gramps to be the rich old guy Danny knew. If Danny hadn't been there to advise him, who knew what might have happened? As Howie had said, time travel made everything *bloomin' complicated*.

For the last few minutes, Howie had been raising his nose to sniff at the air. Now he asked everyone to gather around. He said, "I believe that we are not alone on this island.''

"How do you know?'' David asked.

"I can smell them.''

"You're screwy,'' said Jacob. "Nobody but me knows how to get out here.''

"What one person can figure out, so can another,'' said Elisa.

"Wait,'' said Howie, "there's more. The others are not human.'' He sniffed the air again. "I don't know what they are.''

"Is everybody in the future screwy?'' Jacob asked.

"You don't have to believe me,'' Howie said. "Just keep your wits about you.''

"My wits,'' said Jacob. "Sure. I have great wits.'' He strode off.

"I think we should stay together,'' Elisa said.

They all hurried to keep up with Jacob.

"They smell like lizards. But they must be very large."

"Dinosaurs?" Danny said.

Howie looked at him with surprise and nodded. "Possibly, old chum. Possibly."

Danny looked around and said, "Not much room on this island. They must be awfully small dinosaurs."

"Right you are, chum. Large for lizards but small for dinosaurs."

"I don't smell anything," David said.

Howie traded glances with Danny. Should they tell David that Howie was a werewolf? Danny made a command decision that everybody should be told everything. He said, "Howie's a werewolf."

David asked, "What's that?"

Danny was astonished by David's question, but Howie only nodded and said, "Let's just say I have a lot of dog in me."

"I don't get it."

"You will in a few years when the movie comes out." Howie suddenly called out, "Jacob, Elisa."

The two came back to where Danny, Howie, and David had stopped, and Howie whispered, "We are being followed."

"That again?" said Jacob.

"I'm afraid so. But keep a stiff upper lip. Is the statue much farther, Jacob?"

"Not much." They were walking through a twisting corridor between two masses of impossibly balanced boulders, any one of which could crush a horse. With quick jerks of his head, Jacob studied the boulders. He began to walk again.

A few minutes later they entered a big round area with a flat rock like a stage in its center. Danny was just some kid and not a monster, but even he could feel the strange, ancient power in this place. Important things had been happening here for centuries, perhaps since the dawn of time. The others felt it too. They stepped carefully and were very quiet as they spread out around the central rock and stood looking at it.

"Something is out there," Howie said softly.

They looked at the flat rock for a while longer and then Elisa said, "Where is the dinosaur statue?"

"I don't know," Jacob said. "I left it right here."

"Somebody must have moved it," Danny said.

David nodded and said, "Who's screwy now?"

If the statue wasn't there, it seemed nothing could be done. Yet the kids just stood there without moving, staring at the great flat rock as if they were waiting for something to happen. Danny didn't understand it himself, though he waited along with everybody else.

He heard a small avalanche of pebbles behind him and he swung around in time to see a lime green brontosaurus bound out from behind a boulder. The brontosaurus was about the size of a St. Bernard dog. Then dinosaurs were all around them, none larger than a big dog, and every one of them a fanciful candy color.

Chapter Eight

Bad Luck for the Korb

"They're just like the ghost dinosaurs I saw," Jacob cried.

Danny agreed with him. Except for the fact that these dinosaurs were solid, they were just like the ones he and Stevie had seen back home.

Elisa kept the wary dinosaurs back with lightning bolts she shot into the sky from her fingers. Jacob and David were just as astonished by Elisa's monster ability as they were by the dinosaurs, and they didn't know where to look first.

But it was not long before Elisa's electrical energy petered out. She gave one last crackle, and then backed away blowing on her fingers. Uncertain at first, but with growing confidence, the dinosaurs stepped forward. They were led by a sky blue *Tyrannosaurus rex* who, being about the same height as Danny's father, was the tallest animal in the herd. Did dinosaurs come in herds?

"OK, tough guy," Danny whispered to Jacob, "now's your chance to do your stuff."

Jacob glanced at him horrified and, like everybody else, backed away from the dinosaurs.

Danny felt the central rock poke his back, and he slid up onto it. He and the other kids gathered in the center of it, facing outward, awaiting their doom.

The tyrannosaurus used one of his small delicate hands to motion the other dinosaurs to stay back. He stepped forward and in a voice like an angry radio announcer said, "Who are you and why are you here?"

For a moment Danny and his friends were too surprised to say anything. Danny had heard of miniature animals and even of animals that were funny colors. But outside of the occasional trained parrot, talking animals were rare. Talking dinosaurs, he suspected, were even rarer.

Then Danny mentally gathered himself together and stepped forward. For some reason, a talking *Tyrannosaurus rex* did not seem as frightening as one that was just a slobbering two-legged appetite. Danny said, "We're just a bunch of kids from Brooklyn. And we came to return something. Show him, Jacob."

"It's mine," Jacob said while he eyed the tyrannosaurus.

"Crikey, old man," Howie cried, "you were going to return it anyway. Show it to him."

Jacob looked at the kids and saw they were all thinking the same thing. He pulled the Eye of Brooklyn from his pocket and in a hand that shook a little, held it out to the tyrannosaurus.

An astonished intake of breath came from the dinosaurs, and if the tyrannosaurus had had eyebrows, they would have gone up then. "Where did you get this?" he asked.

Jacob said, "I found it."

"Where did you find it?"

"Here on this island. My island."

Danny thought Jacob had a lot of nerve to say that last, and he was afraid of what the tyrannosaurus might think of it. But the tyrannosaurus only smiled, showing hundreds of sharp teeth. "Why did you take it?" he asked.

Perhaps it was the fact that the tyrannosaurus had the attitude of a schoolmaster or perhaps Jacob's nerve had broken at last, but when he spoke, he whined like a kid who had been caught fair and square and knew it. "I thought it would make a swell shooter. You know, for marbles," he said by way of explanation. His eyes flickered up and back among the dinosaurs. "I didn't know it was yours."

The tyrannosaurus nodded and said, "And you came to return it?"

Jacob nodded once, slowly. "But we can't find the statue it belongs to. The statue was right here."

"Of course you can't find it," the tyrannosaurus said. "When we discovered the Eye missing, we moved the statue to a safer place. We will go there now. Please follow." He turned and the crowd of pastel dinosaurs opened, allowing him to walk through.

"Wait a minute," said Jacob.

The tyrannosaurus turned and looked at him, waiting.

"We don't know who you are. Maybe this doesn't belong to you either." He bounced the Eye in his palm.

"What does it matter? You came to return the stone. We will help you."

"What cheek," Howie muttered, though Danny didn't know whether he was referring to the outrageous nerve of Jacob or of the tyrannosaurus.

Elisa called out, "We would rather destroy the Eye than return it to the wrong person." She took the Eye from Jacob's hand and held it above her head. Danny didn't think she would really throw it—she wasn't the destructive type—but the dinosaurs didn't know that.

The tyrannosaurus walked quickly toward them, waving his tiny hands excitedly. "You must not. I will tell you anything you want to know."

Elisa lowered her arm and put the Eye into her pocket. She said, "Who are you?"

"I am Nemo. And these are my people, the Korb."

"Korb must be another word for dinosaur," Danny said.

"We are not dinosaurs," Nemo said. "We are Korb. Our ancestors came from out there." He lifted his arms and opened them to include the entire sky.

"I don't get it," David said.

"Crikey, old chap," Howie said, "you don't read enough science fiction."

"Enough *what?*" David and Jacob said together.

With astonishment, Danny said, "They must be aliens—creatures from another planet." It made sense. After all, who ever heard of pastel dinosaurs?

"They must be," Elisa agreed.

"Such is the legend," said Nemo. "It is also said that those who crashed here gave us the statue containing what is now known as the Eye of Brooklyn, which created the bog to protect this island."

Elisa said, "And when the Eye is separated from the statue, an imbalance is created causing back luck for everyone?"

"How did you guess?" Nemo asked. He was genuinely mystified.

"We do not guess," Elisa said. "We draw conclusions from evidence."

"Yeah," said Jacob and nodded vigorously.

"Now I get it," Danny cried. "*I* had bad luck. *Jacob* had bad luck, but we couldn't figure out why the draining of the bog was bad luck."

"It is bad luck for the Korb," said Howie. "Without the bog, people would build up the island and the land around it just as they built up the rest of Brooklyn."

Nemo nodded and said, "The Korb would be discovered, which would be the worst luck of all. You see why we must return the Eye of Brooklyn to its socket in the statue."

Howie looked at his friends and cried, "By Jove, this is ripping." He knitted his fingers together and said, "Everything fits. Give him the Eye, Elisa."

Danny was not so certain that Howie was right. After all, nothing had yet been said about time travel or about ghost dinosaurs. Elisa took the Eye from her pocket and was about to hand it over when Danny said, "If we help you, you have to help us." Elisa stopped and looked at Danny with interest.

"How may we do this?" Nemo asked.

Before Danny could speak, they all heard a sound like thunder. It became louder, and in a moment, a herd

73

of ghost dinosaurs galloped through the clearing a few feet above the ground. They ignored the kids, the Korb, the boulders, everything. The herd faded as it approached the other side of the clearing, and soon the thunder faded too. Except that everybody in it was a little shaken up, the clearing was exactly as it had been before.

Breathlessly, Danny said, "You can start by explaining what just happened."

"We have forgotten much that our ancestors knew," Nemo said, and shook his head. "But we do know the shadow herd does not stampede when the Eye is in place."

Elisa nodded and said, "The herd of shadow dinosaurs is more evidence that things are not as they should be. I am sorry, Danny. Whether they help us or not, we must help them. I believe that the future of Brooklyn is at stake." She stepped to the edge of the central rock and handed the Eye of Brooklyn to Nemo. Nemo took it with the care of a person who feared it would break if he looked at it cross-eyed.

Maybe Elisa was right. The Eye, when not balanced by the dinosaur statue, had caused Stevie Brickwald to arrive at Danny's house, caused Theodore Brickwald to arrive at Jacob's house, had made Jacob lose most of his marbles, and had made Danny and his friends travel in time. Not to mention that the bog in two different periods of Brooklyn time had begun to drain. The shadow dinosaurs had not yet hurt anybody, but they were bound to upset people.

Jacob said, "Let's see where you hid the statue." He

leaped from the rock into the midst of the Korb, who backed away to give him room.

"Very well," said Nemo and he set off across the island again. Jacob and the others followed.

As Danny walked along, he said to Howie and Elisa, "Do you think they can help us get home to our own time?"

"I have hopes," Elisa said calmly.

Howie shook his head and said, "The Korb are not much to hang hopes on. I'm not convinced they know what they're doing. The best we can do is keep a stiff upper lip."

"After all," said Danny, "they didn't make the statue or the Eye either. We all could be wrong thinking that just putting the two back together will solve anybody's problems. Maybe you have to recharge the eye somehow before you put it back. Maybe you need a new one every thousand years or so."

"We will find out," Elisa said. "Meanwhile, we must do as Howie suggests and keep our upper lips stiff."

Nemo led them to an area where the ground was sandy red lava that had cooled into rock that was rippled and creased and folded. Craters belched fire and evil-smelling smoke into the air. Everyone sneezed and coughed and tried to wave away the fumes, but to no effect.

Nemo told them to wait. He walked through a curtain of the thickest smoke, and therefore of the most unpleasant smell. A few seconds later he emerged coughing badly, but also carrying the dinosaur statue in his arms like a baby.

With the statue in his lap, he sat gasping on a fold of lava that looked like a saddle, and when he had regained his breath, he carefully examined both the eye and the statue. While the kids and the Korb watched closely, he blew into the socket and buffed the Eye against his scaly hide. Then, like a magician preparing to perform his big trick, Nemo held the eye far away from his body and slowly brought it closer to the statue.

Though he still had doubts about the Korb, Danny had not entirely given up hope that he would soon go home, so he watched carefully as Nemo inserted the Eye of Brooklyn into the statue. Danny expected the Eye to fall out immediately, but evidently Nemo knew the secret method because it did not. Despite his concentration, Danny had evidently missed something; he still didn't see how Nemo had made the Eye stay.

Nemo sat back, relieved, and everybody cheered.

When the shouting died down, Danny said, ''Could you do that again?''

''Do what again?'' Nemo asked.

Danny said, ''Could you take the Eye out and put it back again? I'd like to see how you do it.''

''Why?'' Nemo asked suspiciously.

For a moment, Danny was reluctant to tell Nemo. After all, Nemo seemed pretty possessive about the statue and the Eye. How might he react if he found out that in the future the statue was no longer on the island at all? And then there was all that business about the dangers of telling someone in the past about the future.

Elisa said, ''Why do you wait, Danny?''

Howie said, "Stiff upper lip, old chum. Let time take care of itself."

Danny nodded. Saying that time *ought* to take care of itself and believing that it *would,* were two different things. Still, Danny felt that he had to take a chance. He certainly didn't want Stevie Brickwald in his house forever. He told Nemo about the statue in the attic trunk, about how the Eye had fallen out of it, and how they'd traveled in time.

Instead of being angry, Nemo listened with growing astonishment. When Danny had finished, Nemo said, "Is this all true?"

"We're not screwy," Jacob declared, causing David to laugh.

"Not screwy," Nemo said, and thought for a moment. He said, "It is fortunate that you told us this. David must take the statue and put it into the trunk so that Danny can find it in the future."

David said, "I don't know if we even *have* a trunk like that."

"You must acquire one," said Nemo.

"I *must*?" David asked.

"It is necessary," Elisa said. "We must close the cycle."

"I don't get it," Danny said. "Nemo wants us to put the statue in the trunk now so I can find it later. But if we hadn't found the statue in the future, we never would have come back in time, and none of this would have happened. Where does the cycle begin? Where does it end?"

Elisa said, "If Frankie were here, he would no doubt be able to show you the mathematics of the situation.

I can only guess that the cycle has no more beginning or end than does a knot in a tree. And just as a knot is embedded in the wood of a tree, the cycle is embedded in the fabric of the universe.''

"True," said Nemo. "When speaking of this cycle, the terms *past* and *future* are meaningless.''

Danny looked at the other boys. They all shook their heads at one another and shrugged. Evidently, they didn't understand this any more than he did. Only one thing was certain—that they and Elisa needed to take the dinosaur statue with them.

"What if we don't take the statue?" Jacob asked.

Nemo said, "Perhaps it will arrive at David's house by itself. Perhaps the universe will begin to unravel. Perhaps Danny and his friends will return to the future to find that no one remembers them.''

Elisa said, "I do not care to experiment.''

"I guess not," Jacob agreed.

Nemo removed the Eye from the statue and showed Danny that putting it back required an odd flick of the wrist. It was no wonder that neither Danny nor Jacob had been able to make the Eye stay.

While Nemo carried the statue, Jacob led the way back to the rocky beach where he and the kids had first stepped onto the island. For a minute, everyone looked out at the bog. The sky covered it like a gray metal pot lid. The bog seemed very much the same as it had been on the way out, but in the silence Danny heard soft trickling.

"The water returns," Elisa said.

Nemo handed the statue to Danny, who cradled it in

his arms. Nemo said, "Do not drop the statue into the bog."

"No problem," Danny said and hoped he was right.

The Korb waved and wished them well as Jacob led the kids out onto the bog. The statue seemed to grow heavier with each step, and about a third of the way across, Danny managed to pass it to Elisa who tucked it under her arm like a long loaf of bread.

They had to travel single file, leaving each of them time to think. Danny's thoughts generally centered on his desire to return to his own time and put the Eye back into the statue that had come *out of* the trunk—a much older version of the statue they were about to put *into* the trunk. Screwy.

They had been carried to this time by the Eye and an old photograph. They had an Eye, but no photograph. Danny had no idea how they would go back to the future. He pondered on it, but no idea came. After a while he ignored the nagging question and concentrated on putting his feet into Elisa's footsteps before they filled with water and disappeared.

Chapter Nine

Weird Possibilities

Their return to civilization was not noticed by anyone except a small dog that barked twice at Howie and ran. They walked to David's house while they took turns carrying the statue. Boys called out to Jacob and David, and Jacob asked one of them, "Has anyone seen Theodore?"

"Funny you should ask. We was playing stickball over in front of Sorkin's tailor shop when all of a sudden Theodore gets nervous and says he has to leave, and he leaves."

"Just like that?" asked Jacob.

"Just like that. We accused him of leaving because his mama was calling, but he didn't even turn around to threaten us."

"That's good news," Jacob said when the boy had run off. "Do you think it has anything to do with replacing the Eye?"

"What else could it be?" David said.

There were too many answers to that question so none of them bothered trying to give one.

David's home was an apartment on the top floor of a three-story brick building. The stairway was wide but dim, and was heavy with stale air. Inside, the rooms were large and had high ceilings. The walls and even the ceiling had been papered. Thick white tassels hung from the curtains. The furniture was heavy and made of wood and had clawed feet like the stuff in Zelda Bella's condo. Nobody was there. "Pop's still at work," David said as he laid the dinosaur statue down on the couch.

Television was, of course, far in the future, but Danny did expect to see a radio. When he did not, he asked about it. David proudly showed them a big wooden box on a table in the corner of the sitting room. It had a lot of dials and knobs on the front, along with a set of earphones.

David said, "This is a crystal set I made in manual training class." He turned it on and after it warmed up, allowed each of them to listen through the earphones for a moment. When it was Danny's turn, he heard far-away dance music through a storm of static.

The sound quality was barely lo-fi, and it did not begin to compare with what came through a modern stereo system, but Jacob and David listened to the noise with big smiles on their faces and they commented to each other how good the reception was.

"What's radio like in the future?" David asked.

Once again the question of how much to tell came up. This time it was complicated by Danny's consideration for David's feelings. Telling him how funky and primitive Danny thought the crystal set was would not be kind. Before Danny managed to put together an answer that would be both truthful and polite, Elisa said, "The quality of the sound is much improved, as you might expect, but broadcast principles remain the same."

The answer seemed to satisfy David, and even to please him some. He said, "Actually, I was thinking about building another set, but with two pairs of earphones so that Pop and I can both listen at once."

"Capital idea, old man," Howie said.

"Very modern," Danny agreed, forcing his enthusiasm. Using the crystal set had made him feel homesick, pointing up as it did how far from their own time they really were. He glanced around the room, not quite sure what he was looking for. He would certainly not find a photograph of him and his father. Danny's father would not even be born for many years.

Howie must have noticed how unhappy Danny sounded, or maybe he was not feeling so jolly himself, because he unclipped his tape player from his belt and said, "Time for us to go."

Jacob and David accepted Howie's statement calmly enough but Danny and Elisa looked at him with astonishment. "Of course," Elisa said.

Danny saw what Howie had in mind. They didn't need a photograph. A tape player might haul them into the future just as well. "Will that work?" Danny asked.

"A photograph is not available to us," Elisa said. "But visualizing our own time should be easy. We believe it is there. We have no doubt it exists. We belong there. All we need is something to loosen our

82

tie to this time and we should snap back to our own with ease.''

The way Elisa described it, going home would be easy. ''Sure,'' Danny said happily. ''I don't know why I didn't think of using the tape player.'' He looked down at himself. ''As a matter of fact, we could probably concentrate on any of the stuff we're wearing. It's all from our own time.''

Elisa said, ''The obvious is sometimes too obvious,'' as if that were an answer. ''We must sit on the couch near the Eye.''

''Will it work now that it's connected to the dinosaur statue again?'' Danny asked.

''We can but try,'' Elisa said.

Elisa was right. Yet Danny preferred to hedge his bet a little. He said, ''Look, I'd like to take that Eye out of the statue for just a moment. I'll show you how to put it back.''

''Why?'' asked Jacob.

''Because I was holding it when we came into this time, and I may need to hold it to get back to our time. If everything works the way it did before, the Eye won't travel back with us—it'll stay behind when we disappear.''

''You mean like magic?'' David said.

''No,'' said Elisa firmly. ''Like science.''

''Anyway,'' said Danny, ''we'll disappear and the Eye will fall onto the couch. Somebody will have to put the Eye into the statue so I can find it that way in the future.''

Jacob nodded and said, ''What about it, David?''

''Sounds all right to me.''

Danny loosened the Eye and showed David how to put it back. David tried it and properly inserted the Eye the first time. Danny took it out again and sat down on the couch with it in his hand. Elisa sat on one side of him and Howie sat down on the other. Danny took the tape player from Howie, but he didn't look at it.

Now that leaving seemed possible and in fact seemed very near, he wasn't sure he was ready to go. For one thing, he was not confident he could lift the heavy stack of years between this time and his own. For another, he knew that he would never again see Jacob or David, at least not in their present forms. When next Danny saw him, David would be a wrinkled old guy who gave off a faint aroma of old-fashioned after-shave.

Danny felt a strong urge to take David into the future. They would have a swell time together. But Danny was realistic enough to guess that the swell time would soon end and David would be just as homesick for his own time as Danny was. Besides, Danny's head hurt thinking about the complications caused by growing up with his own grandfather. Would the old guy with the wrinkles still be around, or would he never have existed?

Danny decided to not even suggest David come with them. The possibilities were just too weird.

"I'm ready," said Danny. "Let's blow this Popsicle stand."

They said good-byes all around, and Jacob and David went to sit on the piano bench on the other side of the room.

"We will only disappear," Elisa said, "not explode."

"We hope," Howie said.

" 'Bye, David," Danny said. "See you in a few years. Don't forget what to do with the Eye."

Awed by what was about to happen, David only nodded.

Danny took the Eye in one hand and the tape player in the other. He closed his fist around the Eye and stared at the tape player. He thought of the tapes Howie played in it. He remembered his house and all his friends. He envisioned Gramps as an old man. He believed as hard as he could that his own time existed. The Eye got warm and the tape player grew to fill his entire universe. He felt dizzy and closed his eyes.

When Danny opened his eyes he was kneeling in front of the trunk in his attic. He was holding the photograph in his hand and felt the warmth of the Eye of Brooklyn in his pocket. He looked around quickly and saw Howie and Elisa standing behind him. They all laughed.

"Was that a dream or what?" Danny said.

Howie said, "If it was a dream, old chum, I had it too."

"I also," Elisa said.

"Let's find out," Danny said. He took the Eye from his pocket and walked with it to his room. Stevie was plopped on Danny's bed reading Mother Scary comics. On the cover, a guy without a head was playing the piano.

Without looking up, Stevie said, "You guys give up already?"

"What do you mean, *already*?" Howie asked. "We were gone for most of a day."

"Gone where?" said Stevie. "You were only in the attic for a couple of minutes."

"Very interesting," Elisa said.

"Sure," said Stevie. "Tick-tock. Very interesting."

While Howie and Elisa had been talking to Stevie, Danny sat down on the floor in front of the dinosaur statue. "You guys ready?" he asked.

"Ready for what?" said Stevie.

"Give it a go," said Howie.

Using the peculiar twist he'd learned from Nemo, Danny inserted the Eye of Brooklyn into the eye socket of the dinosaur statue. It stayed. He and Howie and Elisa looked around, waiting for something to happen.

"What's going on?" Stevie asked.

The front doorbell rang.

"You better answer that, Stevie," Danny said. "It's probably your parents."

"What? How do you know?"

"Trust me," Danny said.

Stevie glared at them as he stomped out of the room and ran heavily down the stairs. Danny heard the door open. Stevie cried, "Mom! Dad!"

Howie and Elisa followed Danny downstairs where Mr. and Mrs. Brickwald were having a spirited discussion with their son. Mrs. Brickwald was a thin brittle woman in a pink housedress. Mr. Brickwald wore a hat with a tiny red feather in the band and looked as if he'd slept in his suit.

"But you went away," Stevie wailed. "You *told* me to come here. You even *dropped me off*."

"I don't know, Marge," Mr. Brickwald said.

Mrs. Brickwald looked confused. "Something's going on here," she said. "You go up and get packed."

Stevie gave Danny a dirty look as he ran up the stairs. Politely, Danny asked Mr. and Mrs. Brickwald, "Did you have a nice time?"

"Nice time?" Mr. Brickwald said.

"Wherever you went," Howie said.

"We didn't go anywhere," Mrs. Brickwald said angrily. "I don't even know how we knew Stevie was here."

"Or how we got here," Mr. Brickwald mumbled.

"Is that your car in front?" Elisa asked.

Mr. and Mrs. Brickwald both looked, and when they came back they were not happy. "It is," Mr. Brickwald said. "Did you drive, honeybunch?"

"I did not," Mrs. Brickwald said firmly.

Howie and Elisa sat at the bottom of the stairs while Danny went back to his room to watch Stevie pack. And a good thing it was too. Stevie was about to pack a selection of Danny's comic books.

As Stevie and his parents left, a thin erect man came to the door. He was dressed for golf, but if Gramps was any guide, that meant nothing. The man said, "I'm looking for Mr. Keegan."

"Which Mr. Keegan?" Danny said. "The house is full of them."

"David Keegan," the man said. "I'm his friend, Jake."

Danny looked at his friends. The three of them stared at the man. Danny said, "Jake? Did anyone ever call you Jacob?"

The man laughed. "Not for a long time. Why?"

"Do you play marbles?" Elisa asked.

Jake frowned and said, "When I was a kid I was a demon marbles player. How did you know?"

Quickly, Howie said, "By Jove, you have the hands for it."

"Sherlock Holmes stuff, eh?" said Jake. "Where's Dave?"

Danny led Jake outside, where Gramps was still helping Mr. Keegan put the bookcase together. When Gramps saw Jake, he huffed and puffed as he got to his feet. They shook hands, and Gramps introduced them all around. When he shook hands with Howie, Jake said, "This young man can tell from my hands that I used to play marbles."

"It's kind of a hobby," Howie said.

"Indeed," Elisa said.

To Gramps, Danny said, "We were just about to go for a walk by Dinosaur Bog. Want to come?"

"Leave your grandfather alone," Mr. Keegan said.

"Stuffy, isn't he?" Gramps said. "Sure. I think your father can finish the bookcase alone."

"Thanks," Mr. Keegan said and smiled as he shook his head.

"Come on, Jake. We're going for a walk."

"We have an appointment at the golf course at one."

Gramps said, "There's always time to go for a walk with my grandson and his friends."

As they walked up the street, Danny tried to see Jacob and David in the wrinkled faces and grown-up bodies of Jake and Gramps. It was like looking at an optical illusion. Sometimes the resemblance was enormous. Then Danny would blink and he was sure he was just kidding himself. Of course, learning how to install the Eye of Brooklyn into the dinosaur statue had not been a dream. Jacob and David had been there.

Danny said, "Remember Dinosaur Bog, Gramps?"

"Of course I remember it. It's still there."

"What about Nemo and the Korb?"

"What? Say, what is this?"

"Do you remember?"

"Gee, that sounds familiar," Jake said.

"Yeah," said Gramps. He studied Danny for a moment, then took some time with each of his friends. Gramps said, "I remember kids like you. Jake led us to the island in the middle of Dinosaur Bog." Puzzled, he went on, "But that couldn't have been you. You were just the age you are now."

"I remember something about time travel," Jake said.

Gramps shot him a glance but said nothing.

No one said another word until they reached Dinosaur Bog. They stood with their fingers in the holes of the chain link fence, staring out at the island. The sign announcing the new housing development had fallen over, and as they watched, it sank out of sight, leaving behind only bubbles. After a moment, even the bubbling stopped. It was as if the sign had never been.

"The Korb are safe," Danny said.

"What?" said Gramps. "Oh, sure. I told you everything would be all right, didn't I?"

"Do you remember anything else?"

"Nothing I'd care to talk about at the moment. You kids'll have to trust me."

Danny and his friends nodded. They were willing to go along. Trusting Gramps had been interesting so far.

HOWLING GOOD FUN
FROM AVON CAMELOT

MONSTER BOY	76305-2/$2.95 US/$3.50 CAN
TROLL PATROL	76306-0/$2.95 US/$3.50 CAN
WEREWOLF, COME HOME	
	75908-X/$2.75 US/$3.25 CAN
HOW TO BE A VAMPIRE IN ONE EASY LESSON	
	75906-3/$2.75 US/$3.25 CAN
ISLAND OF THE WEIRD	75907-1/$2.95 US/$3.50 CAN
THE MONSTER IN CREEPS HEAD BAY	
	75905-5/$2.75 US/$3.25 CAN
THINGS THAT GO BARK IN THE PARK	
	75786-9/$2.75 US/$3.25 CAN
YUCKERS!	75787-7/$2.95 US/$3.50 CAN
M IS FOR MONSTER	75423-1/$2.75 US/$3.25 CAN
BORN TO HOWL	75425-8/$2.50 US/$3.25 CAN
THERE'S A BATWING IN MY LUNCHBOX	
	75426-6/$2.75 US/$3.25 CAN
THE PET OF FRANKENSTEIN	
	75185-2/$2.50 US/$3.25 CAN
Z IS FOR ZOMBIE	75686-2/$2.75 US/$3.25 CAN
MONSTER MASHERS	75785-0/$2.75 US/$3.25 CAN

Buy these books at your local bookstore or use this coupon for ordering:

Mail to: Avon Books, Dept BP, Box 767, Rte 2, Dresden, TN 38225
Please send me the book(s) I have checked above.
   My check or money order—no cash or CODs please—for $ _____ is enclosed
(please add $1.00 to cover postage and handling for each book ordered to a maximum of
three dollars—Canadian residents add 7% GST).
   Charge my VISA/MC Acct# _____ Exp Date _____
Phone No _____ I am ordering a minimum of two books (please add
postage and handling charge of $2.00 plus 50 cents per title after the first two books to a
maximum of six dollars—Canadian residents add 7% GST). For faster service, call 1-800-
762-0779. Residents of Tennessee, please call 1-800-633-1607. Prices and numbers are
subject to change without notice. Please allow six to eight weeks for delivery.

Name _____

Address _____

City _____ State/Zip _____

MON 0791

From the bestselling author of
BUNNICULA

JAMES HOWE

Suspense-
filled Mysteries
featuring Amateur Sleuth
SEBASTIAN BARTH

WHAT ERIC KNEW 71330-6/$2.95US/$3.50Can
Sebastian and his friends discover there's more
than a ghost haunting the dark cemetery!

STAGE FRIGHT   71331-4/$2.95US/$3.50Can
Sebastian must unravel ominous messages
and backstage "accidents" before somebody
brings down a *very final* curtain on the glamor-
ous star.

EAT YOUR POISON, DEAR
71332-2/$2.95US/$3.50Can

Sebastian's most baffling case yet!

Buy these books at your local bookstore or use this coupon for ordering:
....
Mail to: Avon Books, Dept BP, Box 767, Rte 2, Dresden, TN 38225
Please send me the book(s) I have checked above.
☐ My check or money order—no cash or CODs please—for $ _____ is enclosed
(please add $1.00 to cover postage and handling for each book ordered to a maximum of
three dollars—Canadian residents add 7% GST).
☐ Charge my VISA/MC Acct# _____ Exp Date _____
Phone No _____ I am ordering a minimum of two books (please add
postage and handling charge of $2.00 plus 50 cents per title after the first two books to a
maximum of six dollars—Canadian residents add 7% GST). For faster service, call 1-800-
762-0779. Residents of Tennessee, please call 1-800-633-1607. Prices and numbers are
subject to change without notice. Please allow six to eight weeks for delivery.

Name _____

Address _____

City _____ State/Zip _____

SEB 0491